W0006343

Riverbend – Riverbend Series
Ciara Knight
ISBN-13: 978-1-939081-42-1

Praise and Awards

To my amazing husband, you make everything possible.

CHAPTER ONE

"**S**hould I bow?" Liam Harrow said as he strutted into Mitchem's office. "I'm in the presence of the great Dr. Mitchem Taylor." He sunk into the oversized leather chair across from his desk.

Mitchem dropped the one-of-a-kind sports pen his assistant, Cynthia, had given him, and eyed his old friend. "If you're just here to aggravate me this morning then I have a meeting."

"Nice try. I caught Ms. Gold in the hall on her way to get us coffee. Your calendar's clear until nine-thirty, just like you have your brunette Barbie doll arrange for you every Friday." Liam leaned back and propped his over-sized feet on the edge of Mitchem's desk. The picture of his comrades from Afghanistan shifted in the macaroni frame his son, Andrew, had made in preschool almost four years ago.

He straightened the other pictures Andrew had put inside the frame, of him in his little league uniform and one of Cynthia, Andrew, and Mitchem at the Sweetwater County Fair. That day flashed in his memory. Still wallowing in grief, Cynthia had peeled him off his couch and demanded he take his son to the fair. If it weren't for her, he'd still be on that couch mourning his late wife. And his son would be without a father. "Cynthia's not a Barbie doll. She's brilliant and organized, and I won't have you harassing the best assistant a boss could ask for. Without her, this place would completely fall apart."

"You mean your life would." Liam arched an accusatory brow at the picture.

Cynthia entered carrying a Riverbend Café coffee in each hand, the town logo proudly displayed on the side of the disposable cups—*Where Dreams Begin...Just Around the Riverbend.* "Good morning, gentlemen." She glided across the floor then gracefully held out a cup to each of them.

Her pianist-like fingers, the tips painted a deep burgundy, grazed Mitchem's thumb. Heat shot through his hand before the warmth of the coffee could even penetrate the cup. He retracted his arm and set the beverage in front of him. "Thank you, Ms. Gold."

Liam took his coffee, holding her hand a second longer than necessary. "Yes. Thank you, Ms. Gold," he mimicked, his tone syrupy sweet.

Mitchem wanted to slap his friend for throwing in a playful smile and wink, not to mention his touching. "Liam, behave or I'll throw you out of my office."

"Not to worry." Cynthia turned, her small hips rotating in a tango-esque dance. "Mr. Harrow will behave or I'll drag him out by his ear like my mother used to do to us."

Liam held up both hands. "Hey, I'm just here to show my support for my oldest and dearest friend during his great day of honor."

"Well, you're half right," Mitchem muttered.

Cynthia grinned, that sweet, welcome home grin that always made his day a little brighter. "Don't forget you'll need to be out of here by five today if you want to make it home to see Andrew, and have time to change before the event."

"You sure there's no way out of this?" Mitchem leaned back in his chair and it groaned in displeasure.

"None," she teased. "Besides, it's an honor. You were chosen for this out of all the professors at Riverbend University." Cynthia perched a hip on the edge of the other leather chair, hands clasped on her lap. The steep pitch of her high heels accentuated her long, toned legs.

"Who are you taking as your guest?" Liam asked.

"I'm going solo." Mitchem opened his laptop to avoid eye contact with the two sets of judgmental eyes on the other side of his desk. "Cynthia, don't forget to send my letter of recommendation to the board about Julia Cramer's acceptance into the nursing progr—"

"Dude, stop avoiding the issue," Liam said. "You know, you never question your *assistant*. She knows more than you do. Listen, it's been four years. Don't you think it's time you started dating again? I'm sorry about Martha, but it's time. You're not an old geezer yet. Tell him." Liam swiveled to face Cynthia, his roaming eyes grazing over her legs.

Mitchem had a sudden urge to throw his briefcase at the man for calling him out, and for his playboy behavior.

Cynthia plucked some invisible dust from the table, keeping her gaze fixed to the floor. "I don't want to butt in where I don't belong, but the board did assume you were bringing someone. There's a *plus-one* on the invitation. It is in your honor, so I don't think you should attend alone." She stood and moved toward the door. "Don't forget you have a meeting with Dr. Montreax at nine-thirty and a ten-thirty interview with a prospective student, a conference call right after lunch and a two o'clock retirement reception for Mrs. Jones. After that, you have a three-thirty call with the director of nursing at the University of Tennessee, and lastly, a five o'clock with Mr. Walton from Allied Health Professions about a joint venture. I've already sent him an email, informing him the meeting will not last more than thirty minutes. You'll have to take that call in the car on your way home."

"You're right. You couldn't manage without her." Liam crossed one leg over the other and his cheeks tightened, warning he was about to say something Mitchem would prefer he didn't. "I think you should take Ms. Gold. She'd be an efficient *plus-one*, and could definitely handle herself with the higher-ups."

Cynthia scooted to the doorway. "If you need anything, I'll be at my desk. I'll have lunch here at eleven thirty, so you can eat in between your student interview and your conference call."

"Thank you, Ms. Gold." Mitchem nodded, but waited for the door to close before rising from his chair. "Are you insane? Why are you trying to make trouble when everything's going so well around here?"

"Is it? I mean, sure, you have a competent assistant, but how long are you going to sit around with that sappy look on your face before you do something about it?"

"This is more insane than when you told me you were taking me cliff diving." Mitchem dropped back into his chair and took a sip of his coffee.

"Ah, you missed out, man. That trip was amazing. And I'm not insane. I'm just trying to get my oldest friend to snap out of it and start living his life. Take a chance, live on the edge for once. You've thrown yourself into work and caring for Andrew, but when are you going to actually do something for yourself?"

"And you think taking my assistant is a good idea? Facing a sexual harassment suit is not my idea of doing something for myself. It's living on the edge of stupidity." Mitchem downed another swallow of coffee before he noticed the flavors of cinnamon and sugar. Cynthia surprised him every Friday with a new special way of fixing his coffee. He didn't really even know what it was. She seemed to work magic in all areas of his life, even with Andrew.

"I think you're exaggerating. Paul, over in the math department, is dating another professor. And they haven't been called into the dean's office yet." Liam did that half-grin thing that usually made women fall at his feet. He apparently hadn't figured out that Mitchem was immune to his charms.

"Yes, well, they're both professors. Cynthia, I mean, Ms. Gold is beneath me. I mean, she's my subordinate." Heat flooded his cheeks.

"Say what you will, deny yourself if you want to, but there's nothing wrong with taking your assistant to an awards dinner. Heck, everyone will probably find it appropriate due to your circumstances and how much she's done for you."

"She has done a lot. If anything, it should be her getting the award."

"See? So, ask her." Liam glanced at his watch. "I gotta run. Nine A.M. staff meeting."

"You'll be late."

"I'm the boss. They can wait." Liam chuckled, but his hand paused on the doorknob. "You know, if I had a woman like Ms. Gold in my life, no job would stand in my way. Now, go ask her before you get too old and ugly. I've seen the way she looks at you. Trust me, she'll go."

He bolted from the office before Mitchem could argue. Not that arguing ever stopped the man from meddling.

"Mr. Taylor wants to see you," Liam's deep voice carried from down the hall. "He's waiting in his office. I think he needs to ask you something."

So much for his oldest friend, he was going to be his deadest friend by the end of the day.

The soft clicks of Cynthia's heels warned of her approach. Mitchem scanned his desk, looking for some viable question he could ask Cynthia, but all he saw was the oriental burgundy and cream rug, leather chairs, and bookcases full of academia. No answer.

Cynthia dipped her head around the door. Her short hair fell over her high cheekbones, the dark strands a stark contrast to her bright eyes. Eyes that could melt a man's soul and make him do stupid things. "Mr. Harrow said you wanted to see me."

"Yes, I wanted to know if you wanted to attend the banquet with me tonight." Stupid things like asking assistants to work functions, or any functions for that matter.

She smiled, but he couldn't tell if it was a pity smile for the widower, or a happy smile for the invitation. The room remained silent a moment too long, and he couldn't take it. "I mean it's a business thing and I'd like to have you there to help represent our department."

Cynthia stepped further into the room. One of her hands rested on the curve of her hip as the other held one of her leather bound classic stories she loved so much. "I see. I'm sorry, but I'm not sure I can cancel my plans for tonight. It's awfully late notice."

Plans? She had plans? A date? Who would she be going out with? Was it Dave from the coffee shop she mentioned the other day? Or Professor Winters from Neuroscience? His stomach rolled at the thought. "I see. Well, I wouldn't want to make you cancel a date or anything. It's okay. I'll invite someone else. I just thought—"

"No date. I just have plans with friends."

"Oh." *Get it together, Mitchem. What the hell's wrong with you?* "Well, I wouldn't want you to cancel on your friends either," he chuckled nervously. "I guess I've been hoping the entire event would be canceled." He shrugged. "Hence, the late notice."

"It's a great honor," she said. "You should feel proud."

"Great," he muttered, his voice cracking like a pre-pubescent boy. He cleared the insecurities from his mind and tried to pull himself together, yet stood there, unable to move. Part of him wanted to go downstairs and punch Liam for putting such an insane idea in his head.

"Don't forget you have a meeting in fifteen. You might want to head out."

"Right." He snagged his laptop off his desk and shoved it into his briefcase then headed for the door. When he was sure his voice was steady, he pushed his shoulders back and lifted his chin. "Okay, I'll see you Monday then," he said, wanting to make a clean exit, even if he'd made a clumsy invitation.

Cynthia spun on her heel, her eyebrows rising. "I hope not. I mean, I planned to see you at lunch. Otherwise, I'll be getting food for an empty desk in your office."

He shook his head. Here she was trying to extend him an olive branch to sooth his ego, but he still wanted to kill Liam and throw himself in front of a train. "Right, right. I'll see you at lunch then." Mitchem shimmied between Cynthia and the hall table to break free of the uncomfortable situation. *Get it together, Mitch.* He was acting like a teenage boy, asking his first girl out.

Rachel Vine, the woman that didn't understand the word no, stood at the end of the hall near Cynthia's desk, one hand on a curvaceous hip. "Ah, so you need a date for your banquet tonight? Good thing I'm here to save the day," she said, her ruby, pouty lips oozing venom.

He halted suddenly and Cynthia plowed into the back of him. He stood there, trapped between the woman who would do anything to have him and the woman he wanted but who didn't want him.

"Have a good day." Cynthia shuffled past before he could even apologize.

Still frozen in place, he stared at Rachel. "I appreciate that, but I think it's best if I go alone. It wouldn't be proper to take someone from the university."

"That's funny. I thought I heard you invite Cynthia."

"Yes. Well, it's business. And no one knows my business better than my assistant."

Rachel slinked toward him. "I'd love to learn more about your business."

"Dr. Taylor, you don't want to keep Dr. Montreax waiting." Cynthia placed *Jane Eyre* into its home on the bookshelf behind her desk.

"Yes, yes. I need to run. Thanks again for the offer, but I think I'll go solo." He bolted down the hall to the elevator, rode it to the second floor then marched to the conference room. Opening the door, he spotted Liam. "You're a jerk."

All eyes flew to Mitchem.

"Ah, you asked the question and didn't find favorable results?" Liam smirked.

"No. I made a fool of myself, and you're a jerk for

putting the idea in my head." Mitchem closed the door and headed back to the elevator for his meeting.

His stomach remained on the second floor even when the elevator arrived at the bottom floor and he headed outside. What had he been thinking? Why would he jeopardize the only constant in Andrew's life? In his life? Besides, they couldn't go on a real date or he'd be fired. Liam could break all the rules he wanted, but Mitchem held himself to a higher standard and he wouldn't lower it. Yes, that was why they shouldn't go together. His chest ached for his poor decision.

Who was he kidding? His chest ached because she'd said no.

CHAPTER TWO

Cynthia crumbled into a red vinyl seat at Othello's, Riverbend University's sandwich shop, then leaned over and rubbed her ankle. It still ached from when she'd tripped over a crack in the sidewalk and nearly broke her neck on the way into the office this morning. "Anna, what am I doing? Am I wasting my life waiting on a man who'll never even notice I'm here?"

Anna quirked a perfectly arched brow and waved her French manicure at her. "True, you've been more patient than most, but you said he asked you out?"

"Yes...no. Oh, I don't know. This is ridiculous. I mean, it's been almost four years, and now that I'm feeling like I can finally move on he asks me to attend a banquet with him? But of course, he only did it out of obligation."

Anna patted Cynthia's trembling hand. "Tell me exactly what he said. Who was there? How did it happen?"

"Liam came by for his Friday morning coffee with Mitch. When I walked in, Liam teased him about inviting me to the banquet. Next thing I know he's asking me to go."

Anna lifted her chin as two men ogled her from three tables over. Eyes were always on Anna Baker. The woman had more beauty than any one person should possess. "Back up. Liam left and then Mitch called you into his office?"

"Yes, if I'm remembering correctly. It all happened so fast, I thought I'd faint from lack of oxygen. But then he said it was business and he should take me because I know everyone, so I don't think he was actually asking me out."

"Don't be so sure." Anna scooted closer. "You know, I think this might be a date in disguise. Think about it. If you reject him then he can't face you every day. Maybe he's tip-toeing around to see if you're interested."

"I told him no."

"You did what?" Anna's normally perfect façade cracked, shattering into a wrinkled look of disgust. "Are you insane? You've pined over the man for almost four years. Why, in your demented little mind, would you say no?"

"Because he didn't really want to ask me. Liam practically left him no choice. What was the man supposed to do? He was only being polite."

"You don't know that," Anna scolded. "I think you're sabotaging. I know you're going to hate me for what I'm about to say, but you need to hear it. You lost everything—parents, baby sister, your ability to have children—all in one car crash. In one instant. But that doesn't mean you have to stop living. Mitch lost his wife and is dealing with his own issues. If you have a shot, and you truly love him, then it's time to stop making excuses. He likes you and you like him. Make this happen."

Cynthia absently rubbed the scar on her belly. Dead skin. Dead womb. Dead hope.

"Even in this fantasy world, where Mitch would want to go out with me, why now? I mean, I finally decided to move on. A better job, a better life. *You* encouraged me to start applying, remember? I can't believe I let my degree sit useless for so long."

"I encouraged you to use your degree, not take a job on the other side of the United States." Anna sighed. "Speaking of, have you heard anything?"

Cynthia shook her head. "No, not yet. It's only been a few days since the interview, though."

"Then why are you freaking out? This is a win-win. March back to that office and tell the man you changed your mind. Go out with him and see where it leads. If it goes nowhere then you know you've made the right decision to move on."

Cynthia's head spun. She'd only applied for jobs outside the state of Tennessee, far away from Riverbend. She knew nothing would change if she remained too close to Mitchem Taylor. "And if it goes somewhere?"

Anna shrugged, her dangling diamond earrings dancing from the movement. Probably a gift from some sheik or prince of an exotic country. "Then you have a decision to make."

Cynthia leaned one elbow on the table. "This

conversation shouldn't be all about me. Why are you here? You could have any man you want, move anywhere you want. Why Riverbend?"

Anna slid her chair away. "You're deflecting."

Cynthia scooted her own chair out and blocked her friend's exit. "And you're avoiding the question."

Anna twisted an auburn curl around her finger. "Because it's a place where dreams begin."

Cynthia smacked her hand. "You can't use the town's motto. That's cheating."

Anna laughed a light, royal kind of laugh. "Perhaps there's a dashing young professor here that I'm in love with."

Cynthia crossed her arms over her modest chest. "You tease."

"Do I?"

Cynthia smiled and shook her head. "You're impossible."

"Yes, and you're a coward. Go out with Mitchem tonight. See if anything happens. And if it does, you can finally relax and enjoy life."

"Cynthia Gold," the man behind the deli counter called.

She tapped her toe against the linoleum checkered floor. "I do enjoy life."

"Sure you do," Anna muttered. "We both know you're not only completely in love with Dr. Mitchem Taylor, but you've become a mother to his son." Anna kissed both of Cynthia's cheeks. "A role you thought you'd never have."

Before Cynthia could reply, Anna fluttered away,

her light fragrance of lilac and roses fading with her exit.

Cynthia maneuvered around the tight space between two chairs to the counter. *Mother.* Her non-existent womb hummed at the thought.

Before she could grab the lunch bag, Sam Dalton rounded the corner and placed a hand over her waiting order. "Hi, Cynthia. How are you today?"

Right on cue, she thought, resisting the urge to roll her eyes. He was always here on Friday afternoons. He was handsome and considerate, but she didn't feel that spark of magic she felt every time Mitch entered the room. Maybe Anna was right. She needed to give up romance novels and chick flicks and live a real life. "Hi, Sam."

"What's wrong? You look like you've got the weight of a life-changing decision on your mind." Sam nudged closer, entering her personal space.

She grabbed her bag of sandwiches resting on the end of the counter and shrugged. "It's Friday. I'm just thinking about my weekend plans." With one glance at Sam, his straight back and bright white smile, she knew she'd opened the door for *the date conversation.*

"Are you trying to decide on which restaurant, or who to take you out?" Sam shoved his hands in his pockets and rocked back on his heels like he always did when he thought he had her cornered.

"Actually, I was thinking about a work event. Oh, speaking of work, I need to go. I've got to get this back to the office. I'll see you later."

"You can count on it." Sam's words followed her

out the door with the promise of another encounter before the end of the day. He was harmless and sweet, but he wasn't taking her subtle hints. She'd have to flat out tell him she wasn't interested next time he tried to ask her out.

She hobbled down the steps then across the annex to the medical building. Students nodded and smiled, knowing that the only way to reach Dr. Taylor about a grade, dropping or adding a class, or to flirt with the attractive man was to get her to approve their entrance. She was the gatekeeper, at least for a little while longer.

Anna was right. She'd say *yes* to Mitchem's invitation. Even if it meant nothing, at least then she could take a chance and finally move on with her life, knowing she didn't miss an opportunity. Armed with his Italian on three-cheese bread, she marched into his office and placed the sandwich on the desk.

Mitchem raised his hand and smiled at her.

She swallowed her pride and fear, and lifted her chin high. "Dr. Taylor, I'd be happy to go with you to the banquet tonight, if the invitation still stands."

"Hello? Mitchem?" a woman's voice called from the speakerphone on his desk.

Heat rushed to her cheeks and her feet wobbled, as though the heels she'd walked in on were suddenly ten feet high. With careful steps, she backed out of his office. Her breath caught in her lungs at her stupidity.

"Who was that?" the woman on the other end of the phone asked.

Cynthia shuffled to her desk and melted into her chair, dropping her head in her hands. "How could I be so stupid?"

"I can't imagine you've ever been stupid." Sam's voice drew her head up. He stood over her, a concerned look creasing his brow. Why didn't she want to go out with him. He was nice, handsome and, most of all, interested.

"What are you doing here?" Cynthia asked, straightening in her seat.

He set Mitch's credit card on her desk. "You dropped this on your way out. I thought you'd want it back immediately, so I brought it to you."

She snatched it and held it tight. "Thank you so much. I can't believe I did that. I'm usually so careful."

"Well, no harm done. Boss doesn't even know." He winked, a playful kind of wink. He stood tall, probably around five eleven or six feet. His blond hair and bright green eyes could have been right off a magazine cover, but nothing stirred inside her.

"Looks like you could use a friend. Why don't I pick you up after work and take you out? I can be your shoulder for an evening. I've been told I have great shoulders." His light, playful tone almost made her feel at ease, but she knew he didn't just want to be friends. He'd been coming around more and more often over the last few months.

She needed to be straight with him. He deserved to find happiness with a girl who wasn't in love with a man she could never have. "Sam, I...I'd love that, but—"

Mitch rounded the corner, briefcase in hand. "I've been called out, but I'll be back in time for my two o'clock. Don't forget I'm picking you up at seven for the banquet." He nodded to Sam before heading down the hallway toward the elevator.

Sam knocked on the top of her desk. "Well, sounds like you've got other plans this evening. I'll catch you later."

For a moment, Cynthia sat alone in the office with only the sounds of distant conversations from the main hall. Her head swarmed and she clutched Mitch's credit card to her chest. Was he just saving her from a bad date? Or did he just want to go as friends? She didn't know what to think, but the one voice in her head that shouted the loudest was Anna's. *Go for it, girl!*

CHAPTER THREE

Mitchem followed the tree-lined, winding road across the river to Cynthia's side of town, his head still swimming with the image of her marching into his office and declaring she'd go with him.

Andrew fiddled with his iPad in the passenger's seat. The one Cynthia had convinced him to get Andrew for educational purposes. When the two of them ganged up on him, he could never say no.

"Dad, can I ask you something?" Andrew asked, his tone hitching to that be-ready-for-a-bomb-to-drop way.

Mitchem swallowed and nodded. "Sure. You can ask me anything."

"Are you going on a date with Ms. Cindy tonight?"

Mitchem's hands jerk and he popped a curb. So much for his years as a rock solid soldier with nerves of steel. "Why would you ask that?"

"Because you look like you're going to choke the steering wheel. Uncle Liam says that you're lonely and it's time for you to move on. That mom's been gone a long time."

Mitchem gritted his teeth, promising he'd give Liam a lashing the next time he saw him. "Don't listen to everything Liam says. He's not even really your uncle."

"I know, but he's nice and I like having him around. He makes you laugh, and that's the only time you sound happy. Well, except when Ms. Cindy's around."

"I'm happy," Mitchem protested.

"Not really," Andrew muttered. "So, do you?"

"Do I what?"

Andrew sighed dramatically. "Have a date with Ms. Cindy?"

Mitchem rubbed his forehead, keeping the other hand on the wheel. "I don't know. It's for work, so..."

Andrew pushed one ear bud into his ear. "But you want it to be a date, right? I'm okay with it, you know. Especially if it's with Ms. Cindy."

"You really like her, don't you."

"She's kind of the only mother I know. I mean, I was so young when Mom died. I feel guilty, but I only really know Mom through pictures and the stuff you told me about. I know she had a soft voice, she was kind and she'd tuck me in at night, but that's it." His voice brightened. "Cindy comes to my ball games when you can't, and brings me home from school when I'm sick. She's like a mom. I don't have one, and she can't have kids, so it'd be a good fit."

She can't have kids? Why did his son know that, but he didn't? "How do you know she can't have kids?"

"Her friend Anna told me. She met us for ice cream once."

Mitchem turned down Cattail Lane and spotted

her house at the end of the street. Why hadn't she ever told him about not being able to have children? Of course, his son could be mistaken, could have overheard her conversation with Anna and misunderstood. Certainly, he'd know if that were the case.

"Ms. Anna came when Ms. Cindy took me to the movies a few weeks ago while you were out of town on business."

"I didn't know Ms. Cindy did those things with you."

"Yup. Uncle Liam thought I should tell you that I was okay with you going out again, that you don't have to stay home with me all the time. He thinks Mom would want you to move on with your life. And he says it's okay that I want a new mom. Do you think that's okay?"

Mitchem glanced at his young son. At nine, he was wiser than most full-grown men. "You know, I'm proud of you. Life hasn't been easy for you, but you're such a good kid."

The flowers Andrew and he had planted as a thank you for babysitting one evening dotted the front bed of Cynthia's home. He'd been here many times, but today felt different. He pulled to a stop in her drive and let out a long breath. "I'll be honest. I'm not sure if I'm ready to go out on a date."

Andrew unfastened his seatbelt and placed a hand on Mitchem's shoulder. "You're ready, Dad. You can do this. But Uncle Liam's right. You better not screw up. There aren't many women like Ms. Cindy who are awesome, yet dumb enough to fall for you." He laughed, a boyish laugh. The kind Mitchem feared would be lost for his son after so much hardship.

"I think you need to hang out with Uncle Liam less. He's rotting your brain." Mitchem opened the door and met Andrew at the front of the car. "Okay, we'll pick up Cynthia then I'll drop you off with the sitter."

"Relax. Your vein's doing the MC Hammer thing again."

Those were words straight from his oldest friend's mouth. No one his son's age even knew who MC Hammer was. "You've definitely been hanging out with Uncle Liam too much. I think I need to find him a woman. One that will stick around more than five minutes."

"But he's fun, Dad. I like hanging out with him. Besides, he knows all the good jokes."

Mitchem halted, his mind going to places he didn't want his nine year old to go. "What kind of jokes?"

"You know, like that utter joke." Andrew hopped up onto the front stoop with wide eyes and a smile.

Mitchem held his breath, not wanting to know what kind of utter joke Uncle Liam had taught him. He crossed his arms over his chest and eyed his son, ready to tell him never to repeat such a joke.

"Why does a milking stool only have three legs?" His son danced between his feet. This was one of those moments that made parents pause and try to assess what's coming. But all they can really do is let it play out.

"I don't know." Mitchem held his breath, waiting.

"Because the cow has the utter."

Mitchem blew out a long sigh. "Okay, that's funny."

Andrew smacked him in the arm. "You thought it was a dirty joke, didn't you. Wait until I tell Ms. Cindy where your mind is."

Mitchem opened his mouth to protest, but the front door swung open and a long leg extended from a waist-to-ankle slit at the side of an elegant black dress. It clung to Cynthia's body in all the right places.

"Dad, close your mouth. You're staring." Andrew giggled then turned to Cynthia. "You look nice, Ms. Cindy."

"Well, I'm glad someone thinks so." She dipped her head and a ringlet glided down her soft, pink cheek. Her partial up-do accentuated her beautiful, long neck and her smoky makeup made her eyes look like sparkling sapphires.

Mitchem's Adam's apple battled with his saliva until he finally managed a swallow he was sure was way too loud. "Yes, you look very nice." What was wrong with him? He saw the woman every day in the office. Though not in a dress that could turn any professor stupid.

"Thank you. Are you ready to go? We need to be there in forty-five minutes." She turned to shut the door. With her back to him, he had a moment to take in all that was Cynthia. Long legs, curves in all the right places, whiffs of floral and something else. A scent he couldn't pinpoint, but it lured him closer with the promise of love and happiness.

Another smack on the arm from his son had him

straightening. He needed to get a grip and quick, before he made a bigger fool out of himself. He wasn't stupid. She'd only accepted his invitation to get rid of the guy at her desk. He'd noticed the stressed tone of her voice, and knew he had to save her, but from what? Had they dated? Was she trying to use him to get back at the guy for something he'd done? Well, if the guy had done something to screw things up with Cynthia, he deserved to be ignored.

Mitchem stepped off the porch and offered his hand so she wouldn't trip in her long gown on the stairs. She secured her purse under her arm, lifted the corner of her dress so the hem rose and took his hand. Her skin, warm against his own, revved his heart and stole his breath.

Her cherry lips parted and she paused mid-step, her eyes transfixed on his. If he didn't know better, he thought she'd gasped, that she'd felt something, too.

Andrew bounced ahead of them. "I don't know how you walk in those shoes. They're so high."

She giggled, a playful sound, full of life that warmed his heart and soothed his soul. "Yes. Well, good thing you're not a lady then. It's kind of expected we wear them for special occasions and sometimes at work."

"My dad makes you wear those every day?" Andrew turned his frown on Mitchem. "Boy, you're a mean boss."

"Wait a second. I didn't assign the dress code. As a matter of fact, I don't believe those kinds of shoes are even expected any more. You can wear sandals, boots, or other low heeled shoes to work. Most of the women in the building don't wear heels anymore."

"So, you don't want me to wear them anymore? They don't look good?" She paused at the car door, waiting for him to open it. He quickly scooted around her and helped her into the car.

"I think they're hot—I mean, of course you don't have to wear them." He shut the door, chastising himself under his breath. Darn Liam. He'd gotten into his head. He'd have to apologize for his remark later when Andrew wasn't around. It wasn't appropriate to say things like that to his assistant.

He settled into the driver's seat and eyed his son in the backseat through the rearview mirror. "Listen, little man. I need to change real quick once we get home. Can you keep Ms. Cindy company?"

"Sure, Dad. I'd love to. I can tell her jokes about—"

"I think we should skip the jokes." Mitchem backed out of the drive. The wrap around Cynthia's shoulder shifted, revealing her delicate, kissable shoulder.

A car honked from behind and he slammed on the brake. "Sorry." He looked behind him once more, avoiding looking at her in fear he'd hit a tree.

"Can I ask you something?" Cynthia asked, her voice low and alluring.

He edged down the drive. "Sure."

"Why aren't you using the backup camera?"

Because every time you're near me lately, I can't think. "I'm still not used to it, I guess."

"But you've had this car for a year," Cynthia reminded him.

Unable to think of a reply, Mitchem shifted the car into *drive* and followed the road over the bridge.

She pointed out the windshield at the town's welcome sign. "You know, when I drove into town the first time, I saw that sign and knew I'd found home." Her voice dropped, a hint of sadness seeping into it.

"The town sign? Oh, you mean the motto."

"Yeah."

"And now?" he asked, not really wanting to know the answer.

"I think this town's still where dreams begin."

He opened his mouth to ask what she meant by that, but couldn't form the words. Something inside him didn't want to know what her dreams were. What if they didn't have anything to do with him? And the thought of her ever leaving Riverbend shredded his insides.

"Are you guys going to dance together?" Andrew piped in. "We're supposed to have a school dance this year and my teacher told me I'd have to dance with a girl. That's just wrong." Andrew wiggled under his seat belt like a captured caterpillar.

Mitchem turned right and followed the main road around the university. "Dance in elementary school? That's awful young."

Cynthia chuckled. "I take it you didn't read the information sheet I left on your home desk last week. It's part of the *Raising Young Gentlemen* program at that expensive school you send him to."

Cynthia turned in her seat and smiled at Andrew. "We've been working on the Waltz, right?"

"Yes, but you're not a girl."

"I'm not? What am I then?"

"You're like a mom."

Everyone sat quiet for a moment. Cynthia slipped a hand over her flat stomach. . "That's the best compliment I've had all day little man. Thanks."

Her hand rubbed her belly another moment. He caught a glimpse of the look on her face. He knew that look, her look of loss. The way she looked when she'd told him about losing her parents and sibling all those years ago. It was true. She couldn't have children.

"So are you going to dance?" Andrew asked again.

Mitchem knew Andrew wouldn't relent. "The banquet's more about talking and less about dancing."

"Translation," Cynthia said. "Your dad doesn't know how to dance."

"That's not true. I'm an excellent dancer."

"Sure you are," Cynthia said with a hint of sarcasm in her voice.

"I'll have you know I took ballroom dancing when I was in middle school. My mother said every young man should know how to dance if they were going to sweep a girl off her feet."

"And has it worked for you yet?"

"Once." He fought the sadness in his voice, but anytime he mentioned his late wife that feeling of loneliness crept into his heart. "Perhaps someday I'll have another opportunity."

They turned down the long winding road to his home at the end of a cul-de-sac. A house too large for just Andrew and himself, but he'd fallen in love with the tall white columns and red brick front. It looked inviting, yet regal at the same time.

"I've always loved this neighborhood. Old homes have such charm," she sighed wistfully.

"Perhaps you'll live here someday."

"No, I don't think so. My scrooge-for-a-boss will never pay me enough."

"Hey, I don't set your salary. If I did, I assure you I'd increase it exponentially. I wouldn't be able to survive without you."

"Me either," Andrew chimed in.

A flash of something crossed Cynthia's face, almost like a shadow of regret. "I'm sure you'd both be fine without me."

Mitchem pulled into the drive and parked then hopped out to open the passenger side door for Cynthia. He offered his hand to help her stand. When she rose in front of him, he knew he should back away to allow her room to get by, but didn't. Instead, he leaned closer. "I don't think we would be," he whispered.

Cynthia's gaze snapped to his. Those blue eyes captured him, and he couldn't move.

The kitchen door at the side of the house flew open, breaking their moment. "You best get a move on, sir. You're going to be late."

"I just have to change, Mrs. Settle. Andrew, be a good host, okay?"

"Yes, sir."

They entered the house through the oversized chef kitchen where Mrs. Settle, his housekeeper, spent most of her time then continued into the living room. "I'll be right down."

"You better be, or you'll miss your own award."

"I'm going. I'm going. Although, I don't know why I'm receiving the award anyway. There are a ton of other professors more deserving."

"Stop your nonsense and get upstairs." Mrs. Settle shoved him up the curved staircase. His tux was already laid out on his bed, pressed and ready to go. He quickly washed his face and combed his hair, all the time remembering Cynthia's beautiful face and knew he was in trouble. How would he ever make it through the night without facing the truth. Liam was right. He couldn't live without Cynthia Gold in his life, assistant or not.

The sound of his son's violin filled the quiet house. The song sounded familiar, but he couldn't quite make it out.

He dressed quickly then hurried down the stairs. At the landing, he paused to watch Cynthia and his son sitting together working on his violin. Andrew lit up every time Cynthia was around. Most of the time he had to pry what few words the little man chose to offer, but when she visited he wouldn't stop talking. Like now, he heard the sounds of laughter and Mitchem's heart warmed. Maybe Liam was right and Cynthia was worth the chance for happiness. After all, how could he deny how well she fit into their lives?

He didn't know if she felt the same, but he did know that he had to take a chance. A chance at a happily-ever-after was worth risking his job, especially if it included his own son's happiness.

CHAPTER FOUR

Cynthia held her breath; waiting for Andy to stumble over the music he termed the 'killer bars'. He drew the bow across the strings and fingered with precision until the final note of I *Will Always Love You*. Pride filled Cynthia at his accomplishment. Not one squeal or wrong note. "That was so amazing! You'll be ready for your solo audition next week for sure. I can't believe you've only been studying for three years. You're a child prodigy for sure!" Cynthia held Andy tight to her chest. Was Anna right? Should she really give this a shot?

"You really think I'll get the solo?" Andy placed his bow and violin into the case with great care.

Cynthia smoothed the small wrinkles from the front of her skirt. "I know you will. And I'll be in the front row demanding an encore."

Andy threw his arms around her. "You're the best. I want you up front with all the other moms and dads."

She hugged him back. A tight hug. A mother's hug.

"Are you ready?"

She fought the tears pooling in the corner of her eyes. Andy could be the only child she ever called her own. The thought of this special little boy being her son filled her with a joy she couldn't describe. But what if Mitch wanted more children? She couldn't give that to him. Was it right to take that chance away from him?

Andy released her and scurried to the living room and his Xbox remote. Mrs. Settle snagged Cynthia's arm. "Just a second. I need her opinion on something."

"You're the one that said I had to rush," Mitch called after them.

The older woman waved dismissively then ushered Cynthia into the kitchen and handed her a napkin. "Okay, spill it. You've got something on your mind and it isn't good."

"I don't—"

"Don't even try it. I've known you since a second after his wife died. And in that second, I saw all your years flash and disappear from your future. Now, I've watched you two dance around your attraction for each other far too long."

"That's a bit dramatic, don't you think?" Cynthia teased.

"Don't try that on me, young lady. I've raised four boys and three girls. I'm way too smart for that. I might be working as a housekeeper and nanny, but I've got years more experience on you."

"I'm not...I just..." Cynthia wrung the napkin until it shredded into bits.

"Oh, my dear lord in heaven. You're going to give up, aren't you?"

Cynthia lifted her chin. "It's been almost four years. Besides, he deserves—"

Mrs. Settle paced the kitchen floor, rounding the island and stopping only ten inches from her. From the way she invaded Cynthia's personal space, she knew the woman was about to scold her in an epic Mrs. Settle kind of way.

Cynthia squared her shoulders and readied for a fight.

The sixty-something woman with frizzy hair stood on her toes and set one hand on Cynthia's shoulders. "Good for you. It's about time that man realizes the fear of losing someone can drive the people who matter most away. Bravo. I think that'll work well."

Cynthia gasped. "I'm not playing games here."

Mrs. Settle lowered back to her heels. "No, dear. I don't believe you are. You're not that kind of girl. But I am." She smiled, a Maleficent kind of smile. "Okay, you better get moving. You're going to be late," Mrs. Settle called to Mitchem from the kitchen.

"I'm ready." Mitchem walked through the door. His broad shoulders and lean waist looked amazing in his tailored tuxedo.

The housekeeper-turned-matchmaker popped one hip out, setting a spotted hand on it. "Yes, I believe you are. Ready for a lot of things."

"What does that mean?" Mitchem asked.

"Just that you're a young man with lots of opportunities in life. You're being honored for your accomplishments, but you still have many possibilities in your near future. You just need to open your eyes to see them before they're gone."

"You feeling okay? You're acting strange." Mitchem

accused.

She leaned against the granite countertop. "Fine, dear. I'm fine. It's others that are clueless."

Mitchem shook his head. "I know you're carrying on about something, but I guess I'll have to wait until we get home to figure it out or we will definitely be late. Am I presentable enough to accept an award this evening?"

"I think you look very studious...and handsome." Cynthia remembered when she'd taken him to have the tux custom made. The man didn't want anything to do with a tailor. She had to practically bribe him with an ice cream to get him into the store. She'd always found it adorable that he would do anything for a sweet.

"You sure we have to go to this thing? All those people there to honor me. For what?"

"I'm not going over this again," Cynthia sighed. "If you're good, I'll take you out for a treat after the banquet."

He smiled, the hidden-secret smile he only showed on occasion. The one that spoke volumes of how much they knew about each other.

"Deal. Okay, little man. Be good for Mrs. Settle."

Mrs. Settle shooed Andy toward the family room. "Oh, he's always good. It's his father that needs some discipline."

Mitchem shook his head and leaned into Cynthia. "I think I've done something wrong. Let's go before I'm sent to bed with no dinner." His warm breath feathered over her earlobe, sending a wave of excitement through her body.

"That'd probably be wise," she said, her voice wobbly and hoarse.

He hovered for a moment, analyzing her with his professor's gaze. She remained poised, ignoring the thousands of four-year old butterflies swooshing around in her belly. "Shall we?"

He nodded and offered his arm. She tucked her hand into the crook of his elbow, thankful there was so much material between them. If not, the butterflies would burst into a raging inferno of excitement.

The evening air brought the fresh smell of magnolia blossoms. The perfumed aroma sweetened her mood with a hint of hope. This evening promised to allow them time outside of the office together, without Andy. A rare chance. She adored Andy, but while she'd mastered parenting, she needed remedial help with romance.

Mitch opened the car door for her. "What are you so deep in thought about?"

She slid into the luxury, leather seats, arranging her gown around her. "Nothing."

With a suspicious glance, he shut the door then walked around the car to the driver's side. The engine revved to life. "I appreciate you going with me tonight. Liam's been after me to start dating, but I'm not sure I'm ready."

She swallowed the sorrow that threatened to burst the words she'd wanted to say for so long. *I'm right here!*

"What do you think?" His words hung heavy in the car between them. Was this her opportunity to confess how she really felt? What if he rejected her? Then she'd take that job she applied for and move. But Anna was right. It was time to know the truth.

She opened her mouth, the words on the tip of her tongue. But one glance his way and the words abandoned her. "I think you'll just have to try and see what happens."

He backed out of the drive using the back-up camera this time. "Is that fair? I mean, what if I'm not ready? I could hurt someone."

The smell of his cologne taunted her with the promise of something wonderful if she scooted closer for a better whiff, but she remained firmly planted in her seat. "There are never any guarantees in love." Something she'd come to realize each time she'd been over to his house for dinner, to play video games with Andy, sitting by the fire with a cup of hot cocoa after she helped Mitch wrap presents late on Christmas Eve. The man had been hopeless with paper and tape.

He sighed and rotated his hands back and forth on the steering wheel. That was when she noticed something. His wedding ring, the golden symbol of his promise to his late wife, was on his right hand. He'd moved it sometime after she'd seen him at work. What had spurred that? "I know Andy deserves a mother," he began, "and I want a woman in my life again, but dating? That world never appealed to me. The thought of even going on one date...I don't know." He crooked a finger inside his bow tie and tugged.

"Strangles you?"

He returned his hand to the steering wheel. "No. It

was never for me. I mean, my wife and I had been friends first. Hung out in a group in high school then we started dating in college. It wasn't like dating though. It sort of morphed from hiking and going to movies with a group, to just the two of us."

"So, you never dated?"

He shrugged. "Well, sure I did. I dated plenty in high school before Martha and I hooked up. A movie with Sarah, a party with Monica, a—"

"I get it. You were a playboy."

Blinding lights flashed through the windshield from a passing car, the driver obviously having forgotten to dim their brights. She shielded her eyes and Mitchem swerved, his hand reached across her body like a barrier from danger.

"Sorry." His hand retreated back to the steering wheel.

"Don't be. You're a father. I'm sure it's a habit," she said, her voice quivering again. What was wrong with her? She'd been alone with Mitch dozens—no, hundreds of times. Why did every look, touch, and whisper send her heart zooming faster than the vehicle they rode in?

He pulled into the parking lot of the Riverbend Conference Center. "I can drop you off up front."

"No, it's fine. I'll walk with you."

"I have to practice if I'm ever going to go on a real date." He followed the road to the front entrance and stopped just outside.

Practice? That was what she was? In the thirty-seconds it took for him to round the car and open the door, her emotions bolted up and down like an amusement park ride, with twists, loops, and drops.

He held out his hand, but she stood on her own, grabbing the doorframe instead. She avoided eye contact. "I'll wait in the lobby. You know, for practice."

"I didn't—"

She shuffled up the front steps, her feet sore from wearing the darn heels all day and now into the evening. But not as sore as her ego. For once, Anna's radar was wrong. He wasn't interested in her, not at all. If he was, he would have made a move by now. No, she was practice for something real. A real girlfriend. Real wife. Real mother to his son. She wasn't any of those things. She was just a fake, an imposter. Her heart constricted with the thought of being a placeholder for the future Mrs. Mitchem Taylor.

"Good evening." Liam leaned down and kissed both her cheeks. "Where's the golden boy?"

"Practicing for a real date," she huffed.

"What?"

"Nothing." She tucked the loose tendril Anna had carefully curled behind her ear. Cynthia could hear her dear friend scolding her from miles away.

"Oh, here he comes." Liam met him at the door. "It's about time, old man. Only you would miss your own award. I thought Ms. Gold here was starting to slip."

She sashayed past them and into the banquet hall. "No. That's all I'm here for, to make sure Mr. Taylor is prepared for his work events."

Liam ushered them ahead. "And you do an

amazing job with such a sack of mess. Now, let's get you seated so we can get this over with. I've got a hot date that I don't want to keep waiting."

Cynthia bit her bottom lip, trapping the words she wanted to say in her mouth. *Can you teach Mitchem how to do that? He doesn't know how to date. He needs some practice.* It was time to move on. This bitter old maid she'd become needed to retire early.

As they maneuvered around the tables, Mitch took her elbow, but she tugged free and plowed into Dr. Montreax. "I'm so sorry. Please forgive me."

"No worries, Ms. Gold. Although, I'm surprised to see you here with your boss. There are rules about dating within departments. Especially a boss and his assistant."

"She's not my date, sir."

"That's right," she bit out. "I'm just here for moral support and practice."

"Relax," Dr. Montreax said. "I was only teasing." He shuffled closer and held her hand up to his lips. "I guess I shouldn't joke. Human resources would have a fit if they heard what I said." The Provost of Riverbend University bowed his head and stepped aside. "We're glad you could join us, Dr. Taylor."

"I apologize for my tardiness, sir."

"Well, no harm done, but we should get started." He disappeared into the crowd Mitch pulled out a chair for Cynthia and then settled into his own spot at her side. Waiters brought salad and bread, filled water glasses, and hovered near by to see to their every need.

Cynthia placed her napkin in her lap. Mitchem's

pinky grazed hers. She froze. He probably just needed something and was attempting to get her attention. Or he dropped something and was about to retrieve it from beneath the table. Still her head swarmed, her stomach tightened, and her heart went tachycardic. Most of all, the heat of his touch radiated up her hand. She looked down to see his finger stroking, touching, teasing her pinky.

She fought for her breath before the corset style dress kept her from ever catching it again. After two stuttered inhales, she managed to raise her chin and look at him. He smiled, but didn't remove his hand. Instead, he covered her hand with his, lacing their fingers.

A deliberate touch.

His deliberate touch.

CHAPTER FIVE

Mitchem couldn't breathe, couldn't talk, couldn't move even when they called him forward. What had possessed him to take her hand? The emotion of the evening? Conversation? The sight of her with his son?

"Dr. Mitchem Taylor," he heard the announcer call once more.

She slipped her hand from his, breaking the moment between them. "Go," she whispered and nudged him from his seat.

Did she think he was being too forward? He concentrated on smiling and nodding, on shaking hands with each of his colleagues. Then he stepped on stage and the applause lowered.

"Dr. Taylor, we are here tonight in your honor," Dr. Montreax said into the microphone. "You were nominated for this award by your staff, the decision voted on by your peers, and the award granted by the Riverbend Awards Committee. And of course, I agreed."

The crowd laughed, but all Mitchem could do was focus on Cynthia, who sat with a smile plastered on her face. He knew that look. It was her politely-escort-a-disgruntle-student-from-the-office look, or her professor-dropped-in-unannounced-so-I'm-going-to-escort-you-out look.

"This award is presented for your outstanding efforts and integrity in educating our future health care professionals," Dr. Montreax continued. "I've read the many papers you've published in medical journals, listened to you speak at conventions, and seen you stay after hours on numerous occasions to help a student or professor through a difficult time. To me, this award stands for more than the words engraved on it. You're an inspiration to us all for breathing life back into a program that nearly lost accreditation four years ago, all while suffering a great personal loss. I believe you are one of the strongest, most competent people I've met. Congratulations! This is well deserved."

The crowd applauded and Mitchem took the podium. From his jacket pocket, he retrieved note cards Cynthia had helped him write a week ago while eating Chinese food and laughing about the way Mr. Nicks from Biology always whistled before he spoke to anyone. He cleared his throat and eyed the cards. The room fell quiet, waiting for his words of wisdom, a professional joke, and well-timed *thank you*. But instead, he laid the cards down on the podium and stared at Cynthia.

Her eyes widened, and he knew she feared he'd crumbled under the eyes of so many colleagues. "I have a speech prepared. It's an amazing speech. I know it's amazing because I had help writing it. Just like I've had help every day in my life. Dr. Montreax spoke about all these amazing things I've done, but to be honest, I didn't do them."

The crowd sat frozen, watching him as if he'd lost his mind.

"I didn't do them alone, anyway," he said and a community sigh echoed in the room. "You see, so many people have helped me along the way. Like Liam Harrow. For the past four years since my wife's death, he's visited me every Friday. A man who some might think of as self-serving and a womanizer."

"Only when it suits my needs," Liam called from the crowd, but Mitchem didn't look at him. He didn't see anyone but Cynthia.

"That might be true, but still, what some of you might not know is that Mr. Harrow did this because he knew my wife and I always met Friday mornings for coffee."

"Awee," several women crooned from the audience. If nothing else, he'd just helped restore some women's faith in a man they all longed to snag, but Liam would probably be the eternal bachelor.

"He wasn't the only one who has been by my side, aiding me not only in academics, but so much more. There's a woman who has stood by my side, typed my notes, altering them so normal people could read them." He snickered at the reality, that she was a walking translator of life for him. "It's not only me, though. I've seen her stay late to help a fellow assistant with a program issue, or cover for a staff member who has a family emergency or health issue. She has gone above and beyond what any professor could ever ask from an assistant. Cynthia Gold is the reason I'm standing before you today. Because of her, I made it through those first six months of darkness when Martha died. She picked up my slack at work, filed the proper paperwork and forms to keep the school of nursing running while I regained my footing, and found a way to work with the accreditation bureau to keep our program open. Because of her, the school is still in session, and I accept this award not just for me, but for all the people around me. Professors, doctors, nurses, students, and assistants, this award belongs to all of you. The achievements that Dr. Montreax so eloquently spoke of are not about one man, but about an entire university, filled with some of the most amazing people anyone could ever hope to work with. Liam Harrow, Dr. Montreax, students, professors, faculty, and most of all, Ms. Gold. This award is for you. Thank you."

Applause erupted, people stood, but he didn't care about them. He cared about Cynthia and the fact he wanted to kiss her, here, now, in front of everyone, but he couldn't. If he did, they'd both be out of a job, so he'd have to resort to holding her hand secretly beneath the table.

Liam stepped in front of him and offered his hand. Mitchem shook it, and twenty other professors and administrators' hands before he finally made it back to his table. But when he got there, Cynthia was gone.

He scanned the crowd while still accepting congratulations until he caught a glimpse of Cynthia's dark ringlet curls and long, breathtaking dress skittering out the door. "Thank you so much. I'm truly honored," he said vaguely to the group surrounding him. Finally, he was able to escape the mass of people and slip out the back to find her. His heart continued to strum a melody of anticipation.

At the outer doors, he saw her exit and jogged after her. In the moonlight, the fabric of her dress glistened. The clip that held her hair up in back glittered like dancing stars. "Cynthia. Where are you going?"

She stopped, but didn't turn. "Home."

He took three long strides, coming to stand just behind her. The beautiful pale skin at the nape of her neck called for his touch, but he shoved his hands in his pockets instead. "Did I say something wrong?"

Cynthia shook her head, but still wouldn't turn.

"Then what is it? Are you mad I didn't use our speech?"

"No. Your impromptu speech was beautiful and heartfelt. Didn't you hear the applause?"

"Yes, but it was for you, too."

She spun, her eyes glistening with unshed tears. He wanted to pull her tight against him and sooth whatever was bothering her. "I know. That's why I need to leave. You were right."

"I don't understand."

She laughed, not in a hysterical way, more of a you-just-don't-get-it kind of way, and he frowned. "You thanked me for all that I've done for you. For all the nights I helped with speeches, or typing, or late night planning sessions."

He couldn't restrain his hands any longer and grasped her arms. "It's more than that. You know that, right? You've walked me through the darkest part of my life. You're like a mother to Andrew. You are smart, giving...beautiful in every way."

She gasped, the tears in her eyes pooling at the corners.

"I know I spoke of business in there, because that's what it was about. But out here it's about more. It's about what could be, between us. What I want it to be."

"Mitchem, Dr. Montreax is looking for you. He wants some photos taken for the Riverbend newspaper," a voice called from the top of the steps.

He released her arms, waiting, hoping she'd say something.

"What do you want it to be?" she asked quietly.

"I don't know, but I'm willing to give it a chance if you are." He held out an arm for her, hoping to escort her back into the building.

"I guess we can talk about it on the way home." Cynthia took his arm, her fingers trembling against his sleeve.

He covered her hand with his, longing to kiss her quivering lips. But not here, not now, not like this. They'd waited so long already, when they finally did it would be perfect. A memorable moment, a real date. Yes, that was what he'd do. He'd plan an amazing night out for them together. Perhaps they could go to Creekside and have dinner, away from prying eyes.

They entered the building once more and Cynthia excused herself to the bathroom while he was ushered off for photos. The moment she disappeared from his sight, he couldn't think about anything but seeing her again. In that moment, he knew that no matter how much he denied it to himself, used the excuse of the university's rules, or hid behind the death of his wife, it was time to let go of the pain of the past. Cynthia Gold was everything he wanted in his future.

CHAPTER SIX

Cynthia paced the hardwood floor, holding her late-afternoon cup of tea in her hand. "Anna, it was like something off of one of those sappy movies you like to tease me about."

"What are you talking about? Slow down. I want details." Anna sat at the dining table in the eat-in kitchen. "Did he kiss you?"

Cynthia retrieved a mug from the cabinet to pour Anna a cup. "I thought you wanted details, not go straight to the good stuff."

"How about you work backwards. Start with the juicy stuff then get to the details."

She poured hot water over a tea bag and the fresh spicy aroma wafted from the water. "You're impossible."

"That's why you love me." Anna batted her eyelashes.

Cynthia placed the cup on the table. "You know that look only works on men."

"Don't be so sure. It's worked on women, too." Anna sipped her tea, her long, dark lashes dipping below the rim of the cup. "So I've been told. Now, spill it."

Excitement shot through her veins at the memory of Mitch's strong hands on her skin. "Okay, on the way to the banquet he asked me if I thought he should start dating. That Liam has been after him for a while to move on with his life. That's when I noticed his wedding ring was on his right hand. He's never moved it from his left hand until yesterday."

"So he kissed you?"

Cynthia sighed. "Do you want me to tell you the entire story or not?"

"Fine. I'll be quiet through the boring details. Go ahead."

Cynthia sat across from her and set her mug on the table, still cupping it so the heat would keep her calm. "Anyway, he said he needed to practice dating. As if that was why he'd asked me to the banquet."

"What a jerk. Okay, I change my mind. It's time for you to move on and give up on that creep."

"Let me finish. It turns out he wasn't practicing. I was his date. At least, I think I was."

"Because he kissed you?" Anna sat forward with both elbows on the table.

"No. He followed me outside after his speech and put his hands on my arms." She stroked her sleeve, where his touch had burned a sense of longing into her. "He told me that it was me he wanted to date."

"He said that?" Anna's eyebrows rose, her attention fully on the story now.

"Yes...well, I think he did. It was definitely implied, though. He said all the things he thanked me for in his speech were professional, but there was more. I'd helped him through a dark time. He loves seeing me with Andy, and he wants to talk about us."

"Then what?" Anna asked.

"Isn't that enough? I mean, all this time I didn't even know if he cared about me as more than just the woman that brought him coffee." Her heart did that skipping routine it had practiced all night in her chest.

Anna stood, her chair scraping against the hardwood floor. "It's plenty."

Cynthia felt like her body lifted from the ground. "So, you don't think I'm reading too much into this? I mean, like you said, he didn't kiss me."

"A man like Mitchem Taylor wouldn't cross a line like that without nudging the perimeter first. Unfortunately, he's one of the few gentlemen left in the world."

"Isn't that a good thing?" Cynthia asked.

"Yes, of course. That is unless you want to speed things up. Do you want to wait another four years for him to kiss you?"

"You are obsessed with kissing. You know that, right?"

"Maybe, but a kiss seals the deal. For a man like Mitchem, it means he's all in. There are no doubts that he'll walk away. If the man gets close enough to get your perfume on his shirt then you're in, girl."

"You're hopeless."

"Maybe, but you're naïve. It's time for you to take control, or you'll be an old spinster before you two get past the conversation stage and tip-toeing around the future."

Cynthia wanted to argue that there was plenty of time. They didn't need to rush. It wasn't like her biological clock was ticking or anything. But she was right. Mitchem was handsome, fit, charismatic, and women flocked to him. The worst part about that was he didn't have a clue. In his mind, he was still off the market and didn't know how to deal with dating. If they were going to have a shot at being something more then she'd have to make things happen.

"I see I can leave you to your thoughts," Anna teased. "But I'm hoping you'll call him and tell him to get over here. Don't wait until Monday morning when you're at the office. You need to show him that there's more to you, that there's more to life than budgets, typing, and coffee runs." Anna rinsed her cup and headed for the door.

"You're leaving me? I thought we could go to a movie, or shopping, or something. You're supposed to hold my hand through this."

Anna flipped her auburn hair over her shoulder and swayed the hips that brought men to their knees. She opened the front door. "Nope. It's time for me to give you some tough love. You figure out what you want, darling, and make it happen. I've held your hand far too long. It's time for you to fly on your own. I'll talk to you tomorrow." About to pull the door closed behind her, she paused. "Call him."

With those last simple words, Cynthia realized how complicated her life was about to get. Still, she straightened, marched to her cell on the side table and opened her contacts, only to crumble onto her couch. Wasn't it the man's job to ask *her* out? What if she scared him off? He probably needed some time to think about things before he called her. Knowing Mitchem, he'd be planning something. He didn't do things on a whim. He calculated, analyzed, and executed. It was part of his charm, that Indiana Jones persona, and she'd always had a thing for the mild Professor Jones that came to life when he left the office.

She lowered the phone to her lap and sat, thinking, analyzing, wondering what to do until she finally managed to find the nerve to dial. The phone went straight to voicemail. She panicked and hung up, as if caller ID wouldn't reveal it was her. She punched the innocent pillow at her side. "Stupid. Come on, Cindy. Get it together."

After four deep breaths, she dialed once more. Again, voicemail answered. "Hi, it's Cynthia. Give me a call today." She hung up without another word. Short, not too much implied. It hopefully wouldn't scare him off, but would give them a chance to talk.

That was strange. She'd never gotten his voicemail when she called on a weekend. Was he avoiding her? Maybe Anna was right. It had been long enough and Mitchem needed a push. Last night opened a door that she refused to let close, even if it meant her embarrassment and ultimate resignation. If need be, she could always leave for one of the jobs she'd applied for thousands of miles away.

She dialed his home number, ready for a battle of wills. Mitchem would undoubtedly scurry around the perimeter of what last night meant, but she wasn't having that. The man needed to realize what he'd lose if he didn't get over himself.

The phone rang once, twice. "Heloooo?"

"Hi, Andy. Is your dad there?"

"No, he's not. Mrs. Settle isn't happy. Dad was supposed to be home in time for her to leave for her niece's baby shower. I told her I'd be fine, but—"

"I'll be right over."

Something was wrong. Mitchem was many things, but an irresponsible parent wasn't one of them. Something was definitely wrong. It had to be if he wasn't answering his phone. She dialed him once more then again and again. She kept redialing all the way to his home.

She pulled into the drive, hoping to find his car, but the driveway sat vacant except for Mrs. Settle's little Honda.

Andy hurtled the front bushes and landed a few feet away. "Hi. It's good to see you." He threw his arms around her and she knew she wanted to spend the rest of her days with this little boy. Even if something happened to his dad, she'd be there for him. *No, don't think such thoughts. Mitchem's fine.*

"Any word from your dad yet?"

"No." Andy shuffled between feet.

"Don't worry. I'm here and we'll have fun while we wait for him to come home. I'm sure his cell just isn't fully charged and he didn't realize it had died. Everything will be fine," she reassured him, but was it? Would everything be okay?

CHAPTER SEVEN

Mitchem ran his finger along the leather spines of *Tale of Two Cities*, *Emma*, and *Pride and Prejudice*. All volumes she had already collected. There had to be something in the old bookshop. By the musty odor, this store had survived the test of time, tornadoes, fires, and the Internet.

"Looking for something special?" Rachel's sultry voice said. For once, he wished Liam was around. Mitch didn't enjoy Rachel Vine's banter and flirting the way Liam pretended to in public.

"Hi, Rachel," he managed, but kept his attention on finding that special gift. He couldn't show up at Cynthia's house without something, a tangible item to show just how much more she means to him than just an assistant. It had to be big, thoughtful, loving.

"You look like you could use a drink to get your mind off of something. How about—"

"I can't. Sorry. I have plans." He pulled a book from the shelf and leafed through the pages as if he actually wanted to know what words awaited beyond the front cover. Despite the fact he'd already seen the play, watched the movie and read the book, *The*

Adventures of Tom Sawyer captivated him more than the woman trying to engage him in a conversation right now.

"Oh, I see. You know, I heard about your speech at the banquet last night. You had a *plus-one* with you." She leaned her bare shoulder against the wall of books in front of him and sucked in a long breath until her breasts were nearly in his face. "Strange taking your assistant to an event like that. You must get sick of seeing her, since you spend all day with her as well."

"No. I could spend all night with her, too." The words tumbled from his mouth before he could think to pull them back.

Her eyes narrowed, and in that second, Mitchem knew she'd make trouble for them. She tilted her head, her gaze drifting around his face, from eyes to chin to cheek then back to eyes. "Well, apparently someone saw a scene out front, a man chasing after an upset woman."

"I hadn't heard, but since I was being honored, I didn't have much time for gossip."

"That's right, you were being honored. You know, if you needed a date, I would've made myself available. I know how rough it's been on you these last few years." Her hand cupped his shoulder and squeezed suggestively.

He replaced the book on the shelf and turned away, her hand falling from his shoulder. He wouldn't let her make a scene.

"You're not looking for a gift for your secretary, are you? I've seen the piles of old dusty books she keeps behind her desk." She snickered and Mitchem's hackles went up in defense.

"She's not my secretary. She's my assistant, and those books are classics."

She slinked to his side once more and shimmied between him and the bookcase. "Well, you better be careful giving your secretary gifts, unless it's Christmas or her birthday. People are already talking after you took her as your *plus-one* to your awards banquet last night. You wouldn't want to lose your job."

"Let them talk." Mitchem rounded the display table and eyed the front door. Unfortunately, it wouldn't be an easy escape since she stood in his direct path. Beyond the large, front glass window, an orange hue streaked across the sky, the only light remaining from the sun. A light in the darkness, that was what Cindy had been to him all this time. Now, she shone bright in his heart and he wanted to feel the heat of her skin, hear the sound of her laugh, live the rest of his life with her by his side.

"You don't mean that. Besides, it's beneath you to date a secretary. Of course, there's nothing wrong with dating beyond your department." Rachel's hand moved to his hip. He sidestepped, but she was too quick for him to pass. "You know, Liam tells me that you're going to start dating again. I know that'll be difficult, but I'm happy to help you. I could even go out with you a few times so you can practice," she rasped.

Did the woman have no shame? He'd rejected her more times than he could count, but still she persisted.

"I don't think I'll need your services any time

soon," he said, his voice fighting to remain calm and clear. "I need to get going. My son needs me."

She moved closer, her face inches from his. Before he could strategize a good exit plan, she wrapped her arms around his middle and pulled him tight against her. "Just know that I'm here if you need me." Her lips pressed to his cheeks then she whispered, "Don't forget there are women out there that'll take advantage of your sweet nature. I'll be around any time, day or night, if you need me." She sashayed around the central bookcase, her blue, hip-hugging dress leaving little to a man's imagination. Not that he wanted his imagination to go there.

He lowered to a chair at the side, waiting a few moments to make sure the woman had left.

It was getting late. He needed to get home and he still didn't have a gift for Cynthia. There had to be a special gift to show how much he cared.

The quiet ride home unnerved him. He missed Cynthia's bright eyes, smile, sweet laugh, and genuine hugs. Knowing he'd have to insist that their dating be kept a secret from the staff broke his heart. Would it make her feel tainted or cheap? Cynthia could never be either. He wanted to shout from the Blue Ridge Mountaintops about Cynthia Gold and how much he cared for her. Had cared for her for years.

He pulled into his driveway to find Cynthia's car and his heart leapt. She was here. If only he had that gift for her. If only Rachel hadn't shown up when she had. The woman never gave up. He hopped from his car with an extra zing of energy. The frogs croaked in unison like some sort of primal love song.

The front door swung open and Cynthia bolted from the top step and threw her arms around him. "Where were you? What happened? You had us all worried. Why didn't you answer your phone?"

The warmth of her body pressed to his stole his breath from his lungs. He held her tight, thanking God for her touch.

She took a deep breath and her arms retreated from him. "You had us worried to death." Her gaze darted about, her face scrunched in terror...no, anger. The lines around her beautiful eyes tightened and her fists clenched at her side. "You weren't hurt, or lost, or passed out somewhere, were you?"

The venom in her voice shocked him. He'd never heard her raise it even an octave before. Always the woman of patience and kindness, but now she looked like she could turn gangster and take him down.

"I went to the book store."

"Bookstore? Really? And why couldn't you answer your phone in the bookstore?"

"My phone?" He reached into his pocket, but his phone wasn't there. "Oh, I must've left it here. I'm sorry. Did you try to reach me?"

"Did I try to reach you? Yes. So did Mrs. Settle, who almost missed her niece's baby shower, and your son who had to worry if you were dead somewhere, leaving him orphaned. I was ready to be a single-mom and raise him, all because you didn't answer your phone, and you didn't even have the decency to call."

"Wait." Had he really forgotten about Mrs. Settle's

niece's baby shower? "I wanted to call... I was at the bookstore because I wanted to—"

She stepped closer, sniffing. "I'm sure I know what you were doing." She shoved past him and jumped into her car. He thought she was going to sideswipe his Audi on her way down the drive, but she didn't. She sped off into the darkness and he was left standing on his front walkway, confused.

"I guess I don't have to yell at you. I could hear Ms. Cindy all the way from my room." Andy stood on the top step.

Mitch slung an arm over his shoulder. "Sorry about that, buddy. I guess I was distracted and forgot my phone, and about Mrs. Settle's niece's shower, too. I should've called."

Andrew shifted from under his arm and pinched his nose. "Geesh, Dad. What's that odor? It stinks bad."

"Odor?"

"Yeah. It's like crazy sweet perfume."

Mitchem closed his eyes and realized that if Andrew could smell it then Cynthia did. That meant he needed something more than a book to show her how serious he was about her.

CHAPTER EIGHT

An overwhelming sense of loss filled Cynthia and she clutched her purse to her stomach. The elevator rose like bile in her throat, but the light scent of Anna's floral perfume settled a calm around her.

"You sure he was out with a woman?" Anna asked, her voice tentative.

"Yes. Like you said, her perfume was all over him. I'm done. I don't know what I was thinking all this time, waiting for a man who will obviously never love me the way I deserve." She let out a sigh. "I received an email offer from the Seattle job and I'm going to take it. It'll be a great experience and a chance at a new life."

Anna bowed her head, a gesture Cynthia had never seen from her confident friend.

Cynthia let out a long breath, lasting the entire ride up two floors. "I'm sorry."

"You don't owe me an apology, but your purse might need one." Anna pointed at the twisted, crunched, and mangled strap.

Cynthia stepped off the elevator and waited for Anna to join her. "It was time for a new purse anyway. A new job, a new life."

"And new friends," Anna mumbled.

"I can't believe I've been dumping on you incessantly for the last two days, and now I'm going to abandon you in Riverbend. You know I'll miss you terribly, but you can come visit me any time you want."

"I'd like that, as long as that new temper of yours calms down." Anna winked.

Cynthia stopped mid-stride, eyeing the doorway where it all started. The office, her tomb of a former life.

Anna stepped in front of her. "I know you're angry with Mitchem, but you realize this will crush Andy. He's already lost one mother. I'm not trying to guilt you into staying. I think it's a great idea for you to start over if Mitchem's truly not interested. Just make sure you tell Andy yourself."

Cynthia swallowed the lump of regret and nodded. "I love that boy. He's probably the reason I stuck around so long, but he's not my son. I have no claim to him, and he deserves a mother that can give him a little brother or sister. If I stay, it'll only torture us both. Over time, I'd be forced to watch Mitchem fall in love, and Andy grow to love a new mother. It would destroy me."

Anna hugged her tight. "I'll do whatever I can to help you through this. You know that."

"I know. But right now, I need to go make that phone call to accept the job, if I haven't lost it already." Cynthia straightened. "Wish me luck."

"I think I'll wish Mitchem luck. He might not make it through the day," Anna chuckled. "I like this new,

I'm-not-gonna-take-crap-from-anyone attitude. Well, except when it's directed at me."

"Then don't tick me off, woman."

Anna's laugh matched her own, and for a second, Cynthia thought she could stay. That her friend would get her through this, but one whiff of Mitchem's sophisticated-professor-meets-adventurous-archeologist cologne left lingering in the office told her it wasn't possible. The memories ran too long and too deep.

She sat at her desk, having decided to call Seattle before Mitchem arrived. Her cell phone showed twenty-two missed calls from him. It didn't matter. He couldn't say anything to change her mind at this point. Even if the woman meant nothing to him, he was ready to start dating, and she wasn't ready to share him.

The phone rang several times before she received the Dean of Humanities' voicemail. "Hello, this is Cynthia Gold. I received your offer for the job and I'd like to accept. Thank you for this opportunity and I look forward to hearing from you." She hit *end* and looked up to find Sam standing in front of her desk, his mouth open.

"You're leaving?"

"Yes, I am." She saw the sorrow in his eyes, matching her own. Sorrow for a love she couldn't have. "I'm sorry I didn't tell you sooner, but I haven't given my notice yet." She clutched the end of the desk and realized she'd avoided this man, not because he wasn't attractive, or nice, or handsome, but because he wasn't Mitchem Taylor. It was time to give other men a chance. To open her heart to the possibility of love. Sam was a great guy. "You know, if that offer still stands, I'd love to meet you for lunch today. I'd like to spend some time with you before I leave."

He gave a half-nod, a shocked smile spreading across his face. "I'll pick you up here at noon. Sound good?"

"Sounds perfect."

Sam left with a little hop in his step. He really was a good guy.

She shuffled a few papers around. At least Mitchem had an early offsite meeting, which allowed her a chance to complete as much in-office work as she could and figure out a way to avoid him during the afternoon.

After completing all her morning work, she typed her letter of resignation and placed it on his desk. Hopefully, she'd be gone before he discovered it neatly stacked at the top of the papers awaiting his signature. She wasn't ready for a fight. More than that, she wasn't ready for him not to care. Emotions nearly crippled her when she'd entered his office. The smell of leather, cinnamon from the candle she'd given him last Christmas, and pure Mitchem Taylor aroma choked her.

The clock chimed noon, and she squared her shoulders then turned to leave, but ran into Mitchem's hard chest.

"Cynthia, I've been trying to reach you. I even drove to your house yesterday and nearly broke your door down. Please, we need to talk about us."

"There is no us." Cynthia moved away, but he grasped her wrist. Her body betrayed her with the heartwarming shot of energy that burrowed into her heart.

Mitchem held her hands tight and leaned down to capture her gaze. "Please, I don't want you to think I chose my job over you, or that the perfume on me the other day was from a date. I wasn't on a date."

Blood swooshed through Cynthia's ears. "You couldn't be reached and you had perfume all over you. What am I supposed to think?"

"Yes, but let me explain. Come, we'll go out for coffee and talk about things. Just give me a chance." He tipped her chin, forcing her to look at him. The minute their gazes locked, she became powerless to pull away. "I've never lied to you before, have I?"

"No," she managed quietly.

"Then come with me. Let's talk about what happened."

Her determination drowned in the sound of her pounding heart that pumped her body full of possibilities. "One cup of coffee."

"Deal."

"Hey, man. I heard you got it on with Rachel. She's blabbing it all over Riverbend." Liam's voice shattered her hope into tiny shards of jagged anger.

Her breath and pulse sprinted to a distant finish line. The room spun under her feet and she thought she'd fall into the one man she never wanted to be touched by again.

"You ready for lunch?" Sam's voice, a beacon of

light to guide her from the clutches of her sorrow with some dignity still intact, boomed in the office. "Sorry for intruding, but no one was at your desk."

"I'm ready. Let's go."

Mitchem held out a hand to keep her from passing. "Wait. We need to—"

"We don't need to do anything. I have a date. I'll be taking an extended lunch, *sir*." She bolted past him and snagged her purse from her desk. The office walls closed in around her, suffocating her with the knowledge that he'd chosen Rachel over her and lied about it.

CHAPTER NINE

Mitchem sat on the edge of his desk, rubbing his temples. "What just happened?"

Liam smacked his shoulder. "I don't know, man, but you don't look so good. You're not really dating Rachel, are you? I mean, don't get me wrong. I have no lost love for that woman, so don't think I'm jealous, but I'm not sure you can handle her."

"I don't want to date, and I don't want Rachel," Mitchem shot back.

"Okay. Then what's the problem? You look almost like you did when..."

The room fell silent. Only the sound of a bird chirping outside filtered through his window. "Like when I lost Martha? That's how I feel. I think I lost my wife."

Liam quirked a you're-crazy brow at him. "I think you need a vacation. Or did you take one to Vegas last night and get hitched in some drunken crazy stunt?"

"No. No. It's nothing like that." Mitchem rounded the desk and lowered into his seat. What had he been doing? Even the other night, he kept her at arm's length. Not just because of school policy, but so that he wouldn't allow himself to get that close to anyone. He wasn't scared of being fired. He was scared of his heart catching fire again. That deep, inexplicable pain that only someone who's lost a loved one could understand. "I think I'm in love."

"With Rachel?"

"No. I'm in love with Cynthia," Mitchem growled.

Liam chuckled. "You finally figured that out, huh?"

Mitchem shook off the fog of regret and eyed Liam. "What are you talking about? You knew?"

"Please. The entire university knows, except you. The woman is amazing. She's been functioning as more of a wife and mother than an assistant for years. Even the Provost asked when you were going to wise up, because he has a perfect job for her now that she has her Master's."

"She does?" Mitchem rubbed his temples, trying to relieve the pounding tension in his head. A white envelope caught his eye and he lifted it to read the contents. *Dear Mr. Taylor, I am tendering my resignation. Consider this my two-week notice.* He gasped. "It's from Cynthia. I guess he offered her the job already. He probably saw us outside the convention the other night."

Liam shrugged. "Maybe, but I don't think so. I only spoke to him this morning."

"I need to go find her and tell her how I really feel, and try to convince her that she's the only woman I want." Mitchem bolted from his seat and made his way to Cynthia's office. Her cell phone rang, drawing his attention to her desk. He knew he shouldn't answer it, but he knew her passcode and had answered it many times before when she wasn't around. He entered the code and hit *speaker*. "This is Ms. Gold's phone. May I help you?"

"Yes, this is Dr. Kraser. I wanted to tell Ms. Gold that I'm excited she's decided to accept our offer. We'll do everything we can to make her feel at home here in Seattle. I just need to know her official start date and what fax number I can send the paperwork to for her to sign."

Mitchem pressed his palms against her desk and braced himself. "Seattle?"

"Yes, I'm sorry. Is this not her secretary?"

"No, I'm afraid not. This is her boss," Mitchem said, wanting to scare the man from ever calling Cynthia again, from ever offering her a position, from ever taking her away from him.

"I see. I'll try Ms. Gold at a later time then. Thank you." The phone clicked off and he lowered to the desk chair, placing his head on the cool wood surface to relieve the pounding heat in his forehead.

"It sounds like you need to win that woman over, or you're going to lose her forever. Go ask her out on a date and pray you can woo her enough to keep her here at the university."

"No. I need to do more than that." He sat up and scanned her work area. There had to be something, some symbol to show how much he loved her, how much he wanted to keep her in his life, but he came up empty. He shot up and the framed picture on her desk fell over with a bang.

Liam stood on the other side of the desk, deep in his own thoughts. The man would help him, he knew that. Mitchem lifted the picture, a copy of the one in his own office of the three of them at the Sweetwater County fair. He didn't know it at the time, but that was their first date. They'd been dating for four years and he'd fallen in love over that time. "I know what I need to do, and it may be the only thing to keep Cynthia here and with me. Will you help?"

Liam smacked the top of the desk. "I'm in! But I hate to be the bearer of bad news. Your girlfriend is on a date with another man."

"I know. That's why I need your help. Also, I think I'll need her best friend, Anna, on my side. Do you think you can explain that Rachel was just playing games and setting me up? That there's nothing between us, and there never will be. My heart belongs only to Cynthia. I'd tell Anna myself, but she's not taking my calls either. For once, Liam, work your charms for the greater good and get her to the County Fair Ground near Creekside this afternoon. And most importantly, make sure she brings Cindy.

CHAPTER TEN

The sound of echoing conversations and the smell of fresh baked bread distracted Cynthia, but not as much as she'd hoped. Everything that had happened in the last few days pinched her head, promising to cause a painful headache at any moment. Usually fresh baked goods would calm any soul, but the scent made her feel nauseous, as if everything in the world had lost its appeal.

"So, you're really leaving?" Sam asked.

Cynthia moved the baked chicken around her plate with her fork, but couldn't manage a bite. "Yes. I'll be moving in two weeks."

"Two weeks? That's fast. You know, I have a cousin in Seattle. I can give you her number so that you'll at least have someone to help if you need anything."

"That's really kind of you." Cynthia set her fork down and dabbed at the corner of her lips.

Sam folded his napkin and put it on his empty plate. "So, what did he do to chase you off?"

Cynthia chuckled, trying to keep it from turning hysterical. "What do you mean? Who?"

"Mitchem Taylor. Your boss. You know, the one

you've been in love with forever. And he's been in love with you." Sam sighed then scooted closer to the table. "I think we've all been in denial, but it's time to face facts. You two are in love, so what are you going to do about it?"

"Love? No. You're wrong. And nothing. I won't be doing anything but leaving for Seattle. You have it all wrong, Sam. Mitchem's involved with Rachel Vine."

"I wanted to believe that rumor, but it's not true. I overheard her talking in the hall to one of her friends. The woman only wanted to break you two up, so that you'd no longer be competition."

A sparkle of hope glistened deep in her soul. "Well, it doesn't matter now. After this many years, it's time for me to move on. I don't want to sit outside his office, answering phones for the rest of my life. I finished my Master's in Literature and Philosophy and I have an opportunity to teach Humanities in Seattle. It's what I've always wanted to do, so I'm not passing that up."

"And you shouldn't. But you shouldn't run away from something because you're scared, either."

She eyed him for a moment. "Sam, I thought you didn't like Mitchem. Now you're trying to get me to miss out on a career opportunity to continue pining away for him?"

"No, I'm telling you to go talk to him, to tell him how you feel and then you can move to Seattle without hanging onto any hope of him. Or you'll discover he feels the same and you'll stay."

She didn't want to admit it, but he had a point. Closure. She needed that, but perhaps a phone call would be sufficient. That way his silver eyes, solid jaw, and dark lashes wouldn't distract her from what she wanted to say. She'd call him when they were done with lunch. Wait, she couldn't. She'd left her cell phone at the office. "Great," she sighed. "I guess I'll have my opportunity to speak with him. I left my cell phone on my desk."

"I think this date is over anyway. Let's go get it. I'll walk you back and hopefully you can talk to him now." Sam held up one finger for the check and the waiter hurried over.

"Please, let me buy lunch." Cynthia reached for her wallet.

"Nope. Even if it wasn't a date, I'm still a gentleman." He dropped some cash on the table, folded the receipt and stood. "Let's get you back to the office."

She followed him across campus, back to the nursing building. As they approached, she saw Anna pacing around at the entrance.

"Where have you been?" Anna called when she spotted them. "And since when do you leave without your cell?"

Cynthia didn't have the energy to defend herself. The day had already taken its toll. "Sorry. What's the emergency?"

Anna snagged her hand. "I'll tell you on the way. I'm not happy with you, though. Who leaves their cell behind? Seriously. I didn't know how to reach you and I was worried you'd flown to Seattle on your lunch break."

"Thanks for lunch," Cynthia called out to Sam as

Anna dragged her to the parking garage.

"Slow down. What's going on?"

"Just trust me," Anna said. She said nothing else on the way to the car, or on the long drive toward Creekside. No matter how many questions Cynthia asked, her friend had gone mute for the first time in their friendship.

Anna pulled into the fairgrounds and memories charged through Cynthia's mind. She fought to keep them at bay, but this was a special place. The first time she'd gone out with Mitchem and Andy. At the end of the day, he'd thanked her for making his son smile, and for lifting the darkness of loss for a few hours. The memory of the way he'd looked at her that day, and the way he'd doctored his son's skinned knee after he'd fallen running to the next ride, it all crippled her with the desire to remain, to keep trying. But it was past time she moved on. "Why did you bring me here? You know what this place means to me."

Anna drove through the opened gate and around the ticket booth to the lake across from where the rollercoaster remained, abandoned, mirroring the way this place made her hollow heart feel. Abandoned.

Several people stood near the shore of the lake. Her stomach lurched, as if an amusement park ride prepared to launch. "What are you up to? I want you to take me back to work, or home, anywhere but here."

Anna stopped, turned off the engine, and looked at Cynthia. "No. I'm your best friend, and I know what's best for you. Trust me. You need to hear him out. Liam told me everything."

"It doesn't matter. It's time to move on, even if he wasn't with Rachel the other night. You were the one who kept telling me I should move on, remember? To stop wasting my best years on a man who'll never commit."

"What are you really afraid of, Cynthia?" Anna took her hand and squeezed.

Cynthia shrugged. "I'm not scared of rejection, if that's what you mean." She'd already been rejected.

"So what is it then? Really?" Anna pushed.

"I don't want to spend the rest of my life not being able to call Andy my son. Never having children of my own, always remaining an arm's length away from happiness. I'd rather lose it than taste it and not be allowed to enjoy it."

"Then go talk to him. He's waiting for you."

Cynthia cleared her throat, trying to keep her emotions under control. "You won't take me back until I do this, will you?"

"Nope."

"I hate you."

"I know."

Cynthia opened the door to the sound of Andy playing on his violin. *I Will Always Love You*, echoed through the empty fairgrounds. The rush of emotion threatened to drop her to her knees in a heap of tears, but she lifted her chin and walked around the car, down the hill to the fence where Liam stood with Mitch and his son. Liam nodded with a knowing-grin then backed up the hill away from them.

"I'm glad you came," Mitchem said, his voice hoarse,

his eyes glistening.

"I had little choice," Cynthia retorted.

"Please. Just listen, and if you still want to leave for Seattle, I'll drive you there myself."

She shot a sideways glance at Andy, but he didn't seem fazed by the comment. "How did you know?"

"Your potential new boss told me. Why didn't you say something about getting your Master's degree?"

She shrugged. "I guess I wasn't ready to let go of my current job. Of you and Andy."

"And now?"

"It's time for me to pursue something else," Cynthia choked.

Mitch stepped closer, taking away her escape route. "I agree."

The violin stopped playing and Andy lowered it to his side. Mitch snagged her hands and she froze. "I want you to better yourself, instead of caring for me and Andy all the time. You deserve nothing but the best, and I'll support you in anything you want to do. I'm sorry that I didn't answer your calls the other night. I'm sorry I let that woman near me. But most of all, I'm sorry that it took me so long to realize how much I love you."

Her body trembled and he squeezed her hands.

"It took me four years to realize I fell in love with you at this spot. When you sat by my side and calmed Andy down after he fell. I've enjoyed every date we've ever been on. The dinners at my house. The late nights of present wrapping. No matter how unconventional our relationship has been, we have dated for way too long." Mitch closed the space between them.

Tears rolled down Cynthia's face. None of this mattered. "We weren't dating. We—"

"I know I said I don't like dating, and I'm not good at it, but that's exactly what we've been doing all this time. Isn't the point of dating so a man and woman can decide how they feel about each other, to know if they have a future together?"

Unable to speak, Cynthia could only nod. Hoping he meant what he said, but she was also scared that he did.

Andy placed his violin in its case and handed something wrapped in white paper to Mitch. "I know you feel like I haven't chosen you over my job, or that I was unfaithful while we were dating, but I'm here to tell you that you are the most important thing in Andy's and my life. I don't need to practice dating anymore. If anything, I've been dating too long."

He handed her the gift. With trembling hands, she peeled the paper to uncover a leather bound edition of *Persuasion* by Jane Austen. "It's lovely."

"It's the story of two people, who've loved each other for years, who finally find their way to each other."

"Yes, I know the story." She opened the book to find a beautiful red, embroidered bookmark that read, *Will you marry me*? On the end, a ring dangled from a gold tassel. A ring with a single solitaire. An engagement ring.

Dr. Mitchem Taylor lowered to one knee in front of his son, Liam, Anna and God. "Cynthia Gold, will you do me the honor of becoming my wife?"

"And my mom?" Andy added, his eyes full of tears, too.

She slid her hand from his and covered her stomach. "No. It's not right. You and Andy deserve more."

Mitch shook his head and crawled forward on his knees to capture her hand once more. "You're wrong. It's us who don't deserve you. I know about the accident and it doesn't matter. With you and Andy, my family will be complete. I don't need any more than that. I don't want any more. All I want is you to say yes. Not because you want to take care of us, or because you think it's your only chance to have a child, but because you love us and want to spend the rest of your life with me."

She looked at them both, scared, happy, excited, unsure, but most of all, in love.

Cynthia searched the landscape, eyeing Liam and Anna in the distance, the rides, the lake, but she didn't find the answer she needed until she returned her attention to Andy and Mitch. At the sight of Andy wiping away tears, she allowed herself to see the truth. This was really happening. "Yes," she choked out. "I'll marry you and be your mom. It's all I've ever wanted."

Mitchem slid the ring on her finger. "Anna helped with the size and the style. If you don't like it, we can return it."

"I love it. And I love you." Cynthia tugged him to standing.

He flung his arms around her, squeezing her to his chest, then Andy's arms wrapped around them both.

After several moments, Mitchem cupped her cheeks

and looked deep into her eyes.
And then he kissed her.

CHAPTER ELEVEN

❝I can't believe I'm shopping for a wedding dress!" Cynthia twirled, the layers of satin spinning around her.

"You look beautiful," Anna choked.

"Don't start, or you'll make me cry. You're next, you know."

Anna shook her head. "Hardly. I don't know anyone that can keep my attention for more than five minutes."

"Liam's been around for years. He's also a handsome young professor. And you two have been awful chummy lately."

"Chummy? What are you, giddy with happiness? Please. The man's a player."

"And you're not?"

Anna sipped her champagne. "No. I'm just selective."

"You keep telling yourself that." Cynthia took a sip of her own champagne. "I better change before Mitch and Andy get here. We need to go for their tuxedo fitting. Then we have to go for a tasting with the caterer. Not to mention, I have papers to grade tonight."

"I can't believe your teaching at Riverbend now. My little friend is growing up," Anna teased.

Cynthia rested her champagne flute on the side table and turned so the sales clerk could help her out of her dress. "Yes, and you know who I have to thank for that? Liam. He put in a good word for me."

"You got that job because the entire university knows you are amazing, and stop trying to insert Liam in every conversation."

Cindy held up one hand. "Okay, okay."

The sales clerk unzipped and peeled her corset style dress from her body. Cynthia quickly threw on her sundress as the clerk carried the dress over and hung it up.

"Where is my beautiful fiancé?" Mitch's deep voice boomed through the small shop.

"Changing so you don't see the bride in her dress before the wedding," Anna said. "It's bad luck, you know."

Cynthia exited the changing room and wrapped her arms around Mitch's middle. "I'm right here."

He leaned down and pressed his strong lips to hers. The world faded into a blur as she lost herself in him.

"Hey, there's a child present." Andy covered his eyes. "You guys aren't going to be kissing all the time, are you?"

"All the time, little man. So get used to it." Mitchem tussled his hair.

Cynthia bent and kissed his cheek, forehead, chin

and nose. Andy blushed. "I didn't want you to feel left out," Cynthia teased.

Andy threw his arms around her. "I'm so happy you're going to be my mom."

"I'm blessed I get a son like you." Cynthia patted his head.

"We need to get a move on." Mitchem ushered them through the door to the car.

"See you later, Anna. I'll be back after our tasting over in Creekside. The Cupcake Lady's providing the cake."

"Yum. I can't wait. See you later."

Mitch drove them through town and down the winding road along the river. At the edge of town, she spotted the sign. "I think we need to change the town motto."

"Why's that?" Mitchem asked.

"Because it should simply read *Dreams Come True in Riverbend*."

"Ah, a philosophical discussion with a fellow professor. I accept that challenge. I like the sign how it is. You see, it's true."

Andy sat forward. "I think you're both right. The dreams come true part is ilplide."

"Ilplide?" Cynthia turned sideways.

"Yeah, when something means something, but it doesn't say it."

"Oh, you mean *implied*. I guess you have a point. I think our son won the debate for you."

"That's our little man." Mitchem held his hand over his shoulder and Andy gave him five.

"So, the town motto will remain. *Where dreams begin...just around the Riverbend.*"

THE END

If you've enjoyed this story please take a second to write a review or tell a friend about what you've read.

For more information please visit
http://www.ciaraknight.com.
Or send her an email at:
ciara@ciaraknight.com

ABOUT THE AUTHOR

Ciara Knight is a USA Today and Amazon Bestselling author who writes 'A Little Edge and A Lot of Heart' that span the heat scales. Her popular sweet romance series, Sweetwater County (rated G), is a small town romance full of family trials, friendly competition, and community love. Also, there is a brand new sister series, Riverbend. The prequel novella is now available on all online retailers, and the first four books will release in 2016.

When not writing, she enjoys reading all types of fiction. Some great literary influences in her life include Edgar Allen Poe, Shakespeare, Francine Rivers and J K Rowling.

Her first love, besides her family, reading, and writing, is travel. She's backpacked through Europe, visited orphanages in China, and landed in a helicopter on a glacier in Alaska.

Ciara is extremely sociable and can be found at Facebook @ciaraknightwrites, Twitter @ciaratknight, Goodreads, Pinterest, and her website ciaraknight.com.